TALES FOR THE
PERFECT
CHILD

Florence Parry Heide

Tales
for the
Perfect
Child

pictures by **Victoria Chess**

A Magnet Book

Florence Parry Heide is an American writer and mother
of five children, and grandmother of five more.
Her books are famous for their wicked wit
and deceptively direct writing.

Victoria Chess is American, a native of Chicago, Illinois.
She is best known for her bizarrely humorous illustrations.

First published in the USA by Lothrop Lee & Shepard Books,
a division of William Morrow & Co., Inc. 1985
First published in Great Britain by Piccadilly Press Ltd 1986
This Magnet edition first published 1988
by Methuen Children's Books Ltd
11 New Fetter Lane, London EC4P 4EE
Text copyright © 1985 Florence Parry Heide
Illustrations copyright © 1985 Victoria Chess
Printed in Great Britain
by Richard Clay Ltd, Bungay, Suffolk

ISBN 0 416 07162 7

These tales are dedicated to
perfect children,
everywhere

F . P . H .   &   V . C .

Contents

TALES FOR THE PERFECT CHILD

Ruby

Ruby wanted to go over to Ethel's house to play. But Ruby's mother said, "You have to watch Clyde."

Clyde was Ruby's baby brother. He had just learned to walk.

"I don't want to watch Clyde. I want to go over to Ethel's house to play," said Ruby.

13

Ruby's mother was tired. She had been
watching Clyde all day. "You have to watch
Clyde because I have to take a bubble bath,"
said Ruby's mother. She went into the
bathroom.

14   Ruby called Ethel. "I'll be over in a minute."

Then Ruby watched Clyde.

She watched him take all of the clothes out
of every chest of drawers in all of the
rooms.

She watched him take all of the rice and all
of the flour and all of the salt and all of the
sugar and all of the coffee out of all of the
kitchen cupboards and spill it all on the nice
clean floor.

She watched him pull the tablecloth off the
kitchen table. The bananas that had been on
the table landed on Clyde's head.

Ruby watched Clyde start to cry very loud.

17

Her mother came out of the bathroom.
"What's going on?" she asked. "I told you to
watch Clyde."

"I was watching him," said Ruby truthfully.
"I was watching him the whole time."

In a few minutes Ruby was ringing Ethel's
doorbell. "I told you I'd be over in a minute,"
she said. "I just had to watch Clyde." 19

Arthur

Arthur liked to wear his old comfortable clothes and his old comfortable trainers. He did not like to get dressed up. He did not like to wear white shirts and nice suits, and he did not like to wear any of the nice ties he had been given for his birthday.

"Arthur," said his mother, "we're going to visit Aunt Eunice. Put on your white shirt and your nice suit and your new tie and your nice new shiny shoes."

Arthur did not want to get dressed up. He did not want to visit Aunt Eunice. He wanted to stay home in his old clothes and watch his favourite programme.

"I want to stay here in my old clothes and watch my favourite programme," said Arthur.

"Well, you're going with me to see Aunt
Eunice, and that's that. And you're going to get
dressed up, and that's that."

Arthur's mother always wanted to tell
Arthur what was what. That was very thoughtful.
Mothers are thoughtful people.

"All right," said Arthur.

Arthur's mother was surprised. Usually
Arthur argued. Arthur was very good at
arguing.

Arthur put on his white shirt and his nice new suit and the tie that Aunt Eunice had given him for his last birthday. He put on the new shiny shoes.

"Now you look like a little gentleman," said his mother.

And he did. He looked like a little gentleman.

As soon as he was all dressed up, Arthur
went out to the kitchen. He opened the
refrigerator. He poured himself a nice big glass
of grape juice. Some of it got on his face, but
most of it got on his white shirt and the pretty
new suit and the tie that Aunt Eunice had
given him for his birthday.   27

Then he went out into the garden. In a few minutes his nice shiny shoes were all muddy.

His mother was sad.

"Oh, dear," she said. "You've spoiled all your nice clothes. You can't go to see Aunt Eunice looking like that. You'll have to stay home."

So Arthur changed back into his blue jeans
and T-shirt and his old comfortable trainers.
His mother went to see Aunt Eunice, and
Arthur had to stay home and watch his
favourite television programme.

29

Gertrude
&
Gloria

Children should be helpful.

That's what Gertrude and Gloria's mother always said. And she was right, just as mothers always are: Children *should* be helpful. They should help with the dishes, for instance. It isn't fair for mothers and fathers to do all the work.

33

"Help clear the table, dears," said Gertrude
and Gloria's mother after dinner.

34   They started to help.

Gertrude carried the dishes over to the
kitchen sink very very carefully.

Gloria was not careful. She dropped the
dishes and broke three plates. Her mother was
not happy.

"Help dry the dishes, dears," said their
mother. "And be sure to put them away where
they belong." Mothers always like to have
everything in the right place. That makes it
easier to find things.

Gertrude dried the dishes very very carefully
and put them just where they belonged.

Gloria put the cups where the plates should
be, and the plates where the pans should be,
and she broke her mother's very best teacup.

Her mother was sad.

She said she would not let Gloria help with
the dishes any more.

Since Gertrude had been so extremely
careful and helpful, and had done such a very
good job, she got to help with the dishes the
next day and every day after that.

Good for Gertrude.

Bertha

It was a lovely, cool, sunshiny day.

"It's a lovely, cool, sunshiny day," said
Bertha's mother. "Stop watching television and
go outside and play."

Bertha did not want to go outside and play.
She wanted to stay indoors and watch cartoons.

"Out you go," said Bertha's mother. "And don't argue."

Bertha wasn't going to try to argue anyway, because Bertha never won arguments with her mother. Mothers usually win arguments. Mothers are bigger than children.

The cartoon was at a very exciting part.

"I'll go outside as soon as I get dressed," said
Bertha.

"Well, hurry up," said Bertha's mother.

"I am hurrying," said Bertha.

45

That was not true. Bertha tried to move
very very slowly. It always took her an
extremely long time to get ready for anything,
especially when she was watching television.

"Hurry up, Bertha," said Bertha's mother.

Bertha had tied knots in her shoelaces so
that it would take a very long time to untie
them. While she untied the knots, she watched
the cartoon.

Bertha put on one shoe. She put the other
shoe in a big vase.

"I can't find my shoe," said Bertha.

"Of course you can," said Bertha's mother.
"I'll help you find it. It can't have walked off by
itself."

What she said was true: Bertha's shoe couldn't have walked off by itself. Bertha's mother had some very sensible sayings.

Bertha's mother looked and looked, but she could not find Bertha's shoe.

"Well, you can wear your old trainers," she said finally. "Here they are. Hurry up and put them on."

"I can't find my jacket," said Bertha.

That was because Bertha had put her jacket
in a very secret place.

Bertha's mother looked and looked for the
jacket. By the time she found it, it had started
to rain.

Bertha settled down in front of the television
set. It was a lovely, cool, rainy day.

Harriet

Harriet was a very good whiner. She practised and practised, and so of course she got better and better at it. Practice makes perfect.

Some children hardly ever whine. Can you believe that? So of course they never get to be very good at it.

"Can I have a piece of that apple pie?"
Harriet asked her mother while her mother
was fixing dinner.

Guests were coming, and her mother
wanted everything to be very nice.

"No, Harriet. The pie is for after dinner.
We're having roast beef."

Children like Harriet are not interested in
roast beef when they are interested in pie.

"I want a piece of pie," whined Harriet. She used her best whiny voice.

"I said no and I mean no," said Harriet's mother. She always liked to say what she meant.

Harriet's mother started to make some nice tomato aspic.

Harriet kept whining, "Can I have some pie, can I have some pie?"

Harriet's mother kept saying that when she said no she meant no. Harriet's mother tried to concentrate on the aspic, but that was very hard to do because Harriet was whining.

Good whiners make it very hard for anyone to think of anything else.

"Why don't you colour in your nice new colouring book?" asked Harriet's mother.

"I want some pie now," whined Harriet.

"Dinner will be ready pretty soon," said Harriet's mother.

"But I want some pie now," whined Harriet.

A good whiner sticks to one subject. A good whiner never gives up.

59

Harriet kept whining, and her mother kept
trying to get dinner ready.

"I want some pie," whined Harriet, and her
mother burned the gravy.

"All right, all right," her mother said. She
was very tired of hearing Harriet whine.

Harriet stopped whining while she had her piece of pie. She always rested up between whines. That's what good whiners always do.

Irving

Irving was visiting his cousin Irma.

Irving did not like to visit Irma. The reason Irving did not like to visit Irma was because Irving did not like Irma. The reason Irving did not like Irma was because Irma always got her own way. The reason Irma always got her own way was because Irma's parents did not like Irma to cry and carry on. And Irma always cried and carried on when she didn't get her own way.

This Saturday afternoon Irma's parents were
planning to take Irma and Irving to a lovely
piano recital at Miss Meesley's house. Irma was
the kind of person who liked piano recitals and
concerts and educational programmes. Irving
was the kind of person who liked football

and circuses and films.

Before they left for the recital at Miss
Meesley's house, Irving said to Irma, "It's too
bad about the bats at Miss Meesley's."

"Bats?" asked Irma, and her eyes grew
unusually large. Usually her eyes were unusually
small. "What bats?" Irma was the kind of
person who was very very afraid of bats.

"I suppose your parents didn't want to tell you," said Irving. "Miss Meesley has a problem with bats this week. Swooping bats. They start to swoop when they hear the music." Irving never cared if he told a lie or not.

"Besides, there's a very good film," said
Irving. "There are no bats in the cinema," he
added.

"Okay," said Irma. "We'll go to the film instead." 69

Irma's parents did not want to go to the
film instead, but Irma cried and carried on,
and so she got her own way.

They all went to the film instead of the
lovely piano recital.

Irving decided he probably liked Irma
better than he'd thought.

Ethel

Emma was kind.

Rose was helpful.

Gladys was very polite.

Harry was the kind of person who *shared*.

And Ethel was a perfect child. You don't
meet many of those.

But then something terrible happened. Ethel
discovered bubble gum. Isn't that awful?

Of course Ethel's mother and father hated
bubble gum. All parents hate bubble gum,
and parents know best.

They didn't like the way Ethel chewed it,
they didn't like the way Ethel popped it,
they didn't like the way Ethel blew great big
beautiful bubbles with it, and they didn't like
the way it stuck to everything.

"We don't ever want to see you chewing
bubble gum again, Ethel," her parents told her.

And they never did.

That doesn't mean that Ethel stopped
chewing bubble gum. Oh, no. But her parents
never *saw* her chewing it.

That's another good thing about Ethel.
Ethel was a very sensible person.

79